Moore man prabhu aas bisvasa

Ram te adhik ram kar dasa.

My heart, Lord, holds this conviction:

Greater than Rama is Rama's servant.

Tulsidas (Ramcharitmanas 7.120.16)

To Anurag, with love

Second Edition, October 2016

anJana
publishing

First Edition, October 2014

Edited by Mudita Chauhan Mubayi

House L, Orient Crest, 76 Peak Road, The Peak, Hong Kong

ISBN: 978-988-12394-1-9

Designed by Jump Web Services Ltd.
Printed in Guangdong Province China
This book is printed on paper made from well-managed
sustainable forest sources.

Amma, Tell Me About

Hanuman!

Part 1 in the Hanuman Trilogy

Written by
Bhakti Mathur

Illustrated by
Maulshree Somani

"Who is your favourite God, Amma?"
Asked Klaka one night, getting into bed.
"Why, our very own Superman!" said she,
"With a heart of gold and a monkey's head!"

"That's not Superman," giggled Kiki.
"I'm quite sure its Hanuman you mean!"
"Yes, it is," said Amma, "but you know,
"He's the first Superman the world has seen."

"He can lift the tallest mountain,
Fly in a jiffy across the mightiest sea.
He can change his form, tiny or huge,
Light as a feather or heavy as can be.

Let me tell you about Hanuman,
And all his adventures as a baby.
There is also a lesson at the end,
Sit tight, listen on and you will see.

A long time ago, in the heart of India
Deep in the forests lived a tribe of Vaanars.
Among them was a happily married couple,
The brave Kesari and the beautiful Anjana.

They had everything they desired;
Well, except for one thing.
They dreamt of having a child,
And the joy it would bring!

So they prayed to Lord Shiva for days,
With the most heartfelt intent.
Shiva was moved by their devotion,
And for Vayu, the Wind God, he sent.

"Anjana and Kesari's dedication pleases me,
Help me make their wish come true.
Bless them with a son of your own being,
With your wisdom and strength, O Vayu!"

Vayu gladly agreed and away he flew,
To find Anjana meditating in the wild.
He whispered his blessing into her ear,
Lo and behold, she was soon with child!

After a few months, she gave birth
To a beautiful baby boy - oh so fair!
With skin the colour of sunset gold,
Round big eyes and pretty curly hair.

Holding him tenderly, Kesari uttered,
"Anjana, he is quite the beautiful one!
Let us name him Anjaneya after you,
Everyone will know him to be your son."

Anjaneya soon grew into a strong little boy,
Born with the blessings of Shiva and Vayu.
And he possessed their godly strength,
Which often caused an accident or two!

One morning, as the sun was rising,
It caught little Anjaneya's eye.
Thinking it was a juicy ripe mango,
He leapt towards it into the sky!

Higher he went and faster he flew,
All the while having so much fun!
Swinging by clouds, whizzing by planets,
Getting closer and closer to the sun.

Having just woken up from his sleep,

The sun was startled by the young fellow.

"What do you want, you imp?" he asked.

The child said, "To eat you, juicy mango!"

Fearing for its life, the sun ran to Indra,
With little, agile Anjaneya in hot pursuit.
"Save me from this monkey," he panted,
"The brat is hungry and thinks I am a fruit!"

The sun pleaded on and on and on, so
Indra rode out on his elephant to see.
He was shocked that the sun was right:
Flying at them was, indeed, a monkey!

"Stop, you impudent beast," yelled Indra.
"Do you think you are very clever?
The sun isn't some snack meant for you,
Eat it and we'll be in darkness forever!"

Seeing Indra on his majestic elephant,
Little Anjaneya was even more excited.
He wanted to play with them both, so
He flew even faster, quite delighted!

Indra mistook the boy's excitement;
"The boy will attack me," he thought.
Brandishing vajra, his mighty thunderbolt,
He hurled it at Anjaneya as his last shot.

Indra's weapon did not miss its mark -
It hit Anjaneya squarely on the chin.
The boy was injured, and quite badly,
He plummeted down to earth in a spin…

Vayu, who arrived at the scene just then,
Was enraged to see Indra assault Anjaneya.
Catching his godson in his arms, he yelled,
"For this cowardly act, Indra, you will pay!"

Vayu flew into a cave with Anjaneya,
Trying his best to undo the harm.
But all his efforts were in vain,
His son lay lifeless in his arms.

"I curse you Indra," shrieked Vayu in rage,
"For harming this innocent boy, my dear son,
I will take all the wind away from the world
Let me see if you find that to be fun."

Vayu sucked away all the air from the world,
Causing breathlessness and chaos everywhere.
Indra knew something had to done quickly,
Or all living things would die for lack of air!

Brahma the creator and Indra rushed
To reason with Vayu and end the strife.
"This was a terrible mistake," said Brahma,
"Let me bring your godson back to life."

"I admit my mistake," said Indra, "Forgive me!"
"Don't punish the world for it, O Vayu.
I bless your son with never-ending life;
Strength, intelligence and divinity too.

And since it was at Anjaneya's chin
That my thunderbolt struck as it sped,
He shall henceforth be called 'Hanuman' -
The one with the distinctive chin," he said.

Hearing all this, Vayu was finally appeased,
So he took a deep breath and blew -
Whoosh! Much to everyone's relief,
Air gushed back to the earth anew.

Now Hanuman became even naughtier,
Causing havoc with his new powers.
One day, he played a prank on a sage,
Flying away with his basket of flowers.

Turning red with anger, the sage cursed him,
"You will forget all your powers from this day!"
Feeling very sorry, Hanuman kneeled before him,
"Forgive me O rishi, I promise to mend my way."

Realising that Hanuman was merely a child,
The sage said, "I cannot undo this, I admit,
But you will recall your powers for a cause
And only when you are reminded of it."

And so it was that Hanuman lost
All memory of his strength and might.
Till years later, he had to help Lord Rama,
But that is a story for another night!

With great power comes great responsibility,
We must help others and not cause harm,
So Klaka and Kiki, act responsibly, or else
You will learn the hard way like Hanuman!"

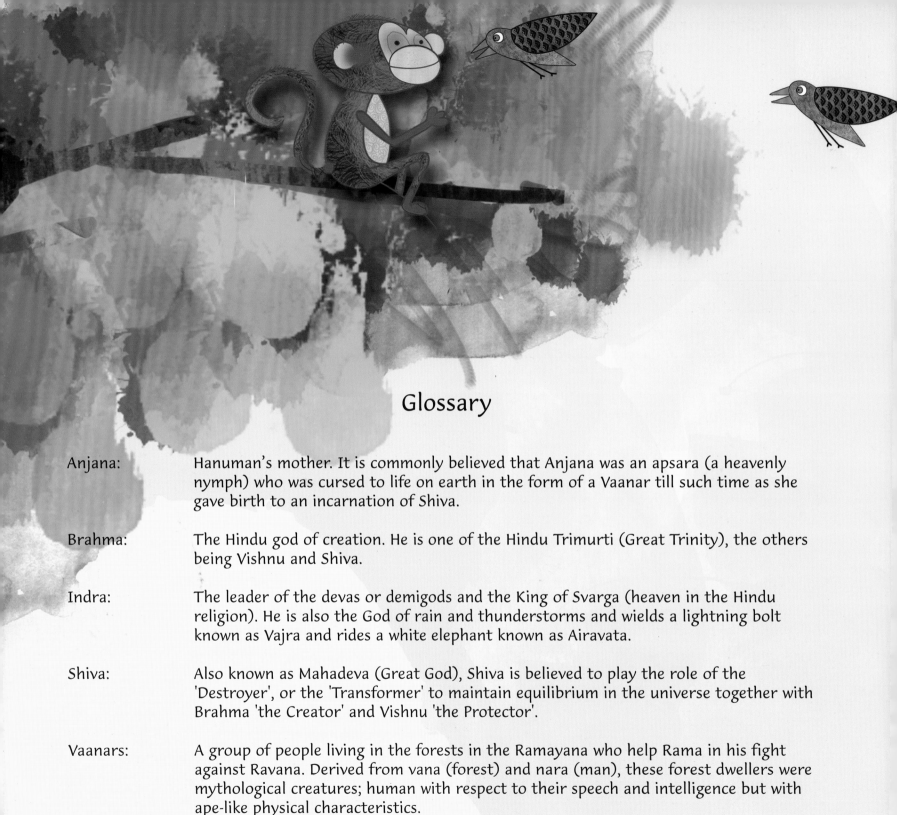

Glossary

Anjana:
Hanuman's mother. It is commonly believed that Anjana was an apsara (a heavenly nymph) who was cursed to life on earth in the form of a Vaanar till such time as she gave birth to an incarnation of Shiva.

Brahma:
The Hindu god of creation. He is one of the Hindu Trimurti (Great Trinity), the others being Vishnu and Shiva.

Indra:
The leader of the devas or demigods and the King of Svarga (heaven in the Hindu religion). He is also the God of rain and thunderstorms and wields a lightning bolt known as Vajra and rides a white elephant known as Airavata.

Shiva:
Also known as Mahadeva (Great God), Shiva is believed to play the role of the 'Destroyer', or the 'Transformer' to maintain equilibrium in the universe together with Brahma 'the Creator' and Vishnu 'the Protector'.

Vaanars:
A group of people living in the forests in the Ramayana who help Rama in his fight against Ravana. Derived from vana (forest) and nara (man), these forest dwellers were mythological creatures; human with respect to their speech and intelligence but with ape-like physical characteristics.

Vayu:
A deva or demigod, who controls the winds and is the spiritual father of Hanuman. Vayu is also known as Pavan and hence Hanuman is commonly called Pavan Putra (son of Pavan).